Danny sucks his thumb. He has sucked it ever since he was a baby. He likes the way his thumb tastes. He feels comfortable and happy with his thumb in his mouth. Then one September day, shortly after school begins, Danny makes a discovery about himself and begins to feel very differently about his thumb.

Totally simple and reassuring, *Danny and His Thumb* can be enjoyed by all children, but will make particular sense to those who have not yet broken the habit.

DANNY AND HIS THUMB

by Kathryn F. Ernst

illustrated by
Tomie de Paola

Prentice-Hall, Inc., Englewood Cliffs, N.J.

To my mother, with love

Danny and His Thumb by Kathryn F. Ernst

Printed in the United States of America • 2

10 9 8 7 6 5 4 3

Prentice-Hall International, Inc., London
Prentice-Hall of Australia, Pty. Ltd., North Sydney
Prentice-Hall of Canada, Ltd., Toronto
Prentice-Hall of India Private Ltd., New Delhi
Prentice-Hall of Japan, Inc., Tokyo

Library of Congress Cataloging in Publication Data
Ernst, Kathryn F
Danny and his thumb.
SUMMARY: As he grows up and starts school, Danny finds he is too busy doing other things to suck his thumb.
[1. Finger-sucking–Fiction] I. De Paola, Thomas Anthony, illus. II. Title.
PZ7.E732Dan [E] 72-8496
ISBN 0-13-196725-8
ISBN 0-13-196808-4 p6k.

Danny sucked his thumb.

He had sucked it ever since he was a baby.

He liked the way his thumb tasted.

He felt comfortable and happy with his thumb in his mouth.

So Danny sucked his thumb whenever his sister took him to the movies,

whenever he had to wait for his mother,

whenever he went for a ride in the car,

whenever he had a haircut,

and when he was just sitting in the back-
yard, thinking.

Danny really liked to suck his thumb.

And the time he liked it best, was at night, just before he fell asleep.

Then one September day, right after school started, Danny decided that he didn't like sucking his thumb as much as he used to.

He didn't like the hard bump he had on
his thumb.

He didn't like to hear his mother say, "Danny, you really shouldn't suck your thumb. It will make your teeth stick out."

He noticed that his best friend, Johnny, didn't suck his thumb anymore.

Amy didn't suck her thumb either. She said that sucking your thumb is silly.

Danny also noticed that he didn't have as much time to suck his thumb as he used to.

He couldn't suck his thumb while he was taking care of his fish,

or learning to read,

or riding his bike,

or blowing out his birthday candles.

He couldn't suck his thumb while he was helping his mother take out the garbage,

or working in the garden with his father,

or talking on the phone,

or singing a song.

He couldn't suck his thumb while he was making cookies,

or painting pictures,

or cutting up his own dinner.

He couldn't suck his thumb while he was holding hands with the boys and girls in his class.

Danny simply couldn't think about his thumb as much as he used to.

He was too busy using his thumb for other things. And he liked the way that felt, being grown-up and busy.

At night when Danny went to bed, he used his thumb to button his pajamas,

to turn out the light,

and to give his mother and father a big hug.

Then he put both hands underneath his pillow, closed his eyes and fell asleep.

After a while the bump on Danny's thumb
went away,

and Danny rarely thought about sucking his thumb again.